Five reasons why you'll love Mirabelle...

Mirabelle is magical and mischievous!

Mirabelle is half witch, half fairy, and totally naughty!

She loves making potions with her travelling potion kit!

Mirabelle loves sprinkling a sparkle of mischief wherever she goes!

She has a little baby dragon called Violet!

If you could have a magical sidekick what or who would it be?

My Daddy would be my sidekick!– Evan

A llama with rainbow coloured skin that can run super fast! – Louis

Sidney, my little Chiuahua will protect me!
– Miss Watchorn

I'd have a dragonfly because they can fly!
– William

A teeny, tiny purple pixie called Emily.
– Phoebe

A giant, flying, rainbow bee! – Erin

A fluffy, cream llama with pink ears! – Miss Jarman

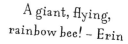

Family Tree

My Mum
Seraphina Starspell

My brother
Wilbur Starspell

My Dad
Alvin Starspell

Me!
Mirabelle Starspell

Violet

Congratulations to Kira,
winner of the Waterstones
competition and named as a
character in this book.

Illustrated by Mike Love, based on
original artwork by Harriet Muncaster

OXFORD
UNIVERSITY PRESS

Great Clarendon Street, Oxford OX2 6DP

Oxford University Press is a department of the University of Oxford.
It furthers the University's objective of excellence in research, scholarship, and
education by publishing worldwide. Oxford is a registered trade mark of Oxford
University Press in the UK and in certain other countries

British Library Cataloguing in Publication Data

Data available

ISBN: 978-0-19-277755-3

1 3 5 7 9 10 8 6 4 2

Printed in China

Paper used in the production of this book is a natural,
recyclable product made from wood grown in sustainable forests.
The manufacturing process conforms to the environmental
regulations of the country of origin.

From the world of ISADORA MOON

MIRABELLE

Has a Bad Day

Harriet Muncaster

OXFORD
UNIVERSITY PRESS

Chapter ONE

'Wheeee!'

It was late-afternoon and I was busy practising my loop the loops in the garden before dinner. Flying on my broomstick is one of my favourite things to do! I love swooping and swirling and feeling the wind whirl through my hair.

'Mirabelle!' called Mum from inside.

'It's dinner time! Dad's made fairy meringue pie for pudding!'

'Ooh!' I said excitedly and immediately flew back towards the ground, landing on the grass with a skid.

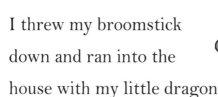

I threw my broomstick
down and ran into the
house with my little dragon
Violet flapping along behind me.

'Did you bring your broomstick in?'
asked Mum as I sat down at the table.

'Oops no,' I said. 'But I promise I'll
fetch it after dinner!'

'As long as you do!' said Mum.
'Broomsticks don't like being left out in
the cold and it's going to rain tonight.'

But by the time dinner was finished
I had forgotten all about my broomstick.
Mum had bought me a new book and I
wanted to read it straightaway. As soon
as the fairy meringue pie was finished

I ran up to my bedroom and snuggled down with Violet to read. The book was *very* good—about a witch who invented a potion that could make your hair turn into sparkling strands of tinsel! I LOVED the idea of tinselly hair! And there was a list of ingredients at the back of the book so you could make the potion yourself! I jumped off my bed before I had even finished the story and collected up all the things I would need, including my travel-size cauldron and laid them on my pillow.

'Mirabelle,' said Mum, poking her head around the door. 'It's past your bedtime!'

'What?!' I had been reading for so long that I hadn't noticed it had got dark outside.

'I just want to make one quick potion Mum before bed. Look, I've already got the ingredients ready!'

Mum glanced at my pillow and frowned.

'Your pillow is not the correct place for potion ingredients,' she said. 'Make sure you clear them up before getting into bed. And there's no time to make the potion now. It's already twenty minutes past your bedtime.'

'Ohhh kaaay,' I sighed. The potion would have to wait for tomorrow. I got changed into my pyjamas, brushed my teeth, and snuggled down into bed to finish my new book by wand light.

I don't use my fairy wand much—witch magic is much more interesting, but it is useful as a torch sometimes. Mum and Dad came in to kiss me goodnight.

'I thought I told you to put your potion ingredients away,' said Mum. 'You can't sleep with them on your pillow like that!'

'I won't,' I promised. 'I just haven't got round to it yet. I'll do it as soon as I've finished this chapter.'

'OK,' said Mum, raising her eyebrows. 'Well make sure you do!' Then she bent down and kissed me goodnight before leaving the room.

I yawned and continued to read my

book, feeling all cosy and cuddly with
Violet.

*'The witch flew across the sky, her silver hair
streaming out behind her like a shooting star.
People down below . . .'*

I yawned again and closed my eyes just
for a moment. It was so comfy lying in
my bed all snuggled with Violet. I could
see the sparkling witch behind my eyelids
now, leaving streaky twinkling trails
in the darkness . . . luring me into the
velvety blackness of sleep.

Chapter TWO

BRRRRRINGGGG!

I jumped awake to the sound of
my alarm. Sun was shining through the
curtains. I rolled over in bed and felt
something sticky on my pillow. What
was it?

'Eww!' I yelped, sitting up in bed and
staring in horror at the puddle of purple

goop on my pillow. Strings of it were clinging on to my hair. Some of the potion ingredients must have spilt out of their bottles in the night and got mixed up in the wrong way!

'Oh no!' I said. 'Mum's going to be cross. She told me to put my potion kit away.'

Hurriedly, I jumped out of bed and covered my pillow with the duvet. I put the cauldron and bottles down on the floor just as I heard Mum approaching my bedroom.

'Good morning, Mirabelle,' she said, poking her head into my room. 'Breakfast in ten minutes or you'll be late for school. Why have you got your witch's hat on already?'

'I umm . . . wanted to see what it would look like with my pyjamas!' I gabbled.

'I just need to have a shower!' Then I shot past Mum and out into the corridor, running as fast as I could towards the bathroom with Violet flapping along beside me. As soon as I got into the bathroom I slammed the door shut and took off the hat. Purple goop dripped off my hair and it was all clumpy and gross and sticky.

'Urgh!' I said as I hopped into the shower and turned it on. It took ages to wash all the goo out. By the time my hair was clean and dried I was late down to breakfast.

'Mirabelle,' said Mum. 'You're going to be late for school!'

'I just like to be super clean,' I said, hurrying over to the cereal cupboard. 'Where are the rose petal fairy flakes?'

'Wilbur finished them this morning,' said Mum. 'You'll have to have some of my batwing porridge instead. It's in the saucepan on the stove.'

'What?' I gasped.

'There's no time to make anything

else,' said Mum.

I took the saucepan off the stove and huffed over to the table where my family were sitting. I thought my brother Wilbur looked very smug with his bowl of half-finished rose petal fairy flakes in front of him. Wilbur and I are both half witch and half fairy but we both hate Mum's witchy food. She likes eating spider-sprinkled toast and caterpillar bolognaise and . . . bat-wing porridge. Yuck! Dad's fairy food is much nicer.

I spooned some porridge into my bowl and squirted lots of honey on it to hide the taste. Then I sat down at the table with a big sigh.

'What's the matter, Mirabelle?' asked Mum, looking at me suspiciously over the rim of her cauldron-shaped coffee mug. 'What mischief have you been up to this time?'

'I'm just having a bad day,' I said.

'Already!?' Dad exclaimed, looking at his watch. 'It's only half past eight!'

I couldn't tell Dad or Mum about the goop in my hair, or about the mess on my pillow—they would only say it was my own fault for not putting away my potion ingredients before I went to sleep, so instead I said, '*Wilbur* took the last of the fairy flakes!'

'*Wilbur* was down here for breakfast ages ago,' said Mum.

'You snooze you lose,' said Wilbur under his breath. I glared at him crossly

and stuck my spoon into my horrible
bat-wing porridge.

I was late leaving the house for school and
Wilbur was cross with me because it meant
he would be late to his wizard school too.
Mum and Dad let us fly to school on our
own, but we must fly together until we
get to the edge of the forest. Then we are
allowed to go our separate ways towards
our different schools.

'Hurry up, Mirabelle,' he said as I
rummaged in the understairs cupboard.

'But I can't find my broomstick!' I
wailed.

'Didn't you put it away last night?' asked Mum. 'I asked you to bring it in after dinner. Don't you remember?'

I did remember.

'Oh no!' I said, running out into the garden with Violet flapping along behind me. The grass was soaked and there were puddles all over the ground.

There was my broomstick lying sadly on the grass with its twigs all damp and covered with leaves.

'It's all wet!' I said to Mum.

'Mmm,' said Mum.

'Hurry up, Mirabelle,' said Wilbur impatiently. 'I've got a wizard spell test this morning and I don't want to be late.'

I stared up at Mum in dismay and she looked back down at me.

'There's nothing for it, Mirabelle,' she said. 'You'll have to ride on that soggy broomstick.'

'Please could I use yours instead?' I pleaded.

Mum looked shocked.

'Absolutely not!' she said. 'Mine is an extremely expensive *designer* broom as you well know! I can't possibly trust you to look after it until you learn how to look after your own things.'

'But Mum . . .' I begged.

'I'm sorry, Mirabelle,' said Mum. 'But you'll have to ride your own. Now you really must be off. It's not fair on Wilbur to make him so late.'

Sighing, I got onto my broomstick and Mum gave me a kiss on the cheek.

'I hope your day improves,' she said. 'Just think about things a bit more before you do them and I'm sure it will. Goodbye, witchlings!' Then she swished inside the house.

Wilbur and I rose up into the air. It was a cold and windy day. I could feel the dampness from my broomstick seeping through my tights and it made me shudder.

'Come on, Mirabelle!' shouted Wilbur. 'We need to fly extra fast!'

'I'm trying!' I said, holding on tightly to my wet broomstick. It wasn't working

quite as well as usual. It was very slow
and it kept juddering about. I hunched
down onto my broom and willed it to go
as fast as it could.

'Come ON!' I growled.

Finally, the broom stopped juddering
and started to fly a little faster. I rose

34

higher into the air and followed Wilbur
who was zooming along in front of
me, the silver stars on his wizard's hat
glinting in the morning light. Why did
everything always go so well for Wilbur?
He never seemed to get into the kind of
trouble I did.

We were almost at the edge of the forest when my broomstick started to misbehave again. I held on tightly as it did a nosedive and then started to shudder along a metre or so above the ground.

'What are you doing?' called Wilbur
from way up above. I couldn't reply. I was
too busy trying to hold on! Suddenly my
broom gave one last almighty shake and
I found myself flying off it, right into a
deep, muddy puddle.

SPLASH.

Hoots of laughter came from above and I looked up to see Wilbur clutching his tummy and rocking sideways in the air. I glared up at him and stamped my foot, which only made more water splash up my legs. My whole uniform was soaked and covered in mud!

'STOP laughing, Wilbur!' I shouted but Wilbur didn't take any notice. Big brothers are SO annoying! And to make everything worse, little drops of water kept showering over my head. I turned around to see my broomstick shaking itself vigorously, trying to get dry. I guess it REALLY hadn't liked being left in the garden overnight. I felt a tiny bit bad and vowed to dry and polish it properly when I got home.

Chapter THREE

By the time I arrived at Miss
Spindlewick's Witch School for Girls,
I was feeling very soggy and sorry for
myself. I landed on the black tarmac of the
playground with a skid and looked around
for my best friend Carlotta, but she was
nowhere to be seen. I guessed she must
already have gone inside. I *was* a bit late

after all. I walked through the big, heavy arched doors and down the echoey, shiny corridor to my classroom.

'Oh, there you are, Mirabelle,' said Miss Spindlewick when I entered the room. 'You're late!'

'I know,' I said. 'I'm sorry, Miss Spindlewick. I . . .'

But then I stopped. What could I say? I didn't want to admit that the reason I had got up late was because I hadn't put my potion kit away before bed, or that my broomstick wasn't flying properly because I had left it out in the rain. Instead, I shut my mouth and tried to look innocent.

Miss Spindlewick crossed her arms over her chest and looked at me disapprovingly.

'I've marked you down as late,' she said, 'which means you can stay in at morning break and sort the new spell books into alphabetical order in the library.'

'But . . .' I began.

'AND,' continued Miss Spindlewick, 'you can run along to Mrs Newt in the lost property office and change into something clean and dry. What in the name of leaping frogs has happened to your clothes?'

I opened my mouth to explain but then shut it again quickly. Miss Spindlewick can be quite fierce when she's cross. I shuffled backwards out of the door and along the corridor to the lost property office. I kicked the wall crossly as I went, doing it a little bit too hard by mistake.

'Oww!' I said, clutching my toe and hopping the rest of the way. This was turning out to be the worst day ever. EVERYTHING was going wrong!

'Morning, Mirabelle,' smiled Mrs Newt when I reached her office. 'Oh, you look a little bit worse for wear today. Fall in a puddle did you? I thought you were quite a good broomstick flyer!'

'I *am!*' I said, feeling crosser than ever.
'It wasn't my fault. It was my broomstick.
It was too wet to fly properly.'

'Oh?' said Mrs Newt, looking
confused. 'Why on earth was it wet?'

'It doesn't matter . . .' I said quickly.
'Please can I look in the lost property box?
Miss Spindlewick says I have to change.'

'Of course dear,' said Mrs Newt. 'It's
over there.'

It took me a long time to find
something to wear from the lost property
box. Everything I pulled out of the box
was either too big or too small or not the
right shape for me. In the end I found

myself wearing one long sock and one short sock and a dress that dragged along the ground. I felt very silly as I walked back along the corridor, holding up the dress so that I didn't trip over it. I saw Miss Spindlewick's mouth twitch when I re-entered the classroom and as I walked towards my desk I could hear little titters and sniggers from all over the room. I made sure to give all the other witches dark glares as I passed them.

'They'll be sorry!' I thought. 'Tomorrow

when I turn up to school *early*, on a completely dry broomstick, with beautiful, tinselly hair. No one will be laughing then.'

I sat down on my chair and looked to my right. Where was Carlotta? I turned to mine and Carlotta's other friend, Kira. 'Hey, Kira,' I whispered. 'Do you know where Carlotta is?'

'She called in sick this morning,' Kira whispered back,

Oh no, I thought, feeling my heart drop right back down into my boots again. I slumped down on my desk and put my head in my arms. Today really was AWFUL!

Things hadn't got any better by lunchtime. I realized that in my hurry to leave the house I had forgotten my packed lunch. Dad always makes me special fairy sandwiches so that I don't have to eat the witch food at school. Today at the canteen it was spider stew. Ugh! I could hardly eat any of it.

In the playground, I couldn't join in with the game of witch-tag because my dress was too long, and there was no Carlotta to keep me company either. I sat on one of the benches and stroked Violet crossly. I think I might have stroked her a little too hard because she squirmed away and then started to blow fire at me whenever I tried to pick her back up again.

'Fine!' I huffed.

We were learning potions in the afternoon and I was partnered with Kira. She's so nice, but she doesn't like to mess around in lessons like Carlotta.

'Today witches, we will be learning a transformation potion,' said Miss Spindlewick. 'This potion will temporarily turn anything it touches into a frog! It is excellent for self-defence.'

My ears pricked up at the sound of that. A transformation potion

51

sounded fun! Maybe my day was about to improve. I picked up one of the bottles we needed to use for the potion and tried to tug the top off it. It was very stiff.

'Let me do it, Mirabelle,' said Kira, kindly.

'That's OK, I can do it,'
I said, straining harder to
pull the top off.

POP!

A load of green fizzy powder spilt all
over the desk.

'Mirabelle!' hissed Kira.

'Sorry,' I said, putting the bottle
down and stepping away from the desk.
Maybe it would be better if I didn't touch
anything else today. I sat back down on
my chair and watched as Kira happily
made the potion on her own. Kira is
excellent at potions! And it *was* quite
entertaining watching my pencil case turn
into a frog and hop around the desk for

five minutes. Even better, at the end of the lesson we were each allowed to fill a small bottle of our potion to take home. I slipped mine into my dress pocket. By the time the bell rang for home time I wasn't feeling *quite* so awful. Still, I couldn't wait to run out of school as fast as I could and jump back onto my broomstick. It was almost dry now and much easier to fly. I whirled into the air, feeling the wind whip round my face and swirl through my hair.

Chapter FOUR

I started to feel a lot better as I flew along, letting the breeze wash away all the horrible and annoying things that had happened that day. I was the sparkling witch Mirabelle! A shooting star whizzing across the sky! And I was going to make sure that nothing else bad happened from now on! I felt *almost* back to my usual self again by the time I spotted Wilbur in the sky, waiting for me by the edge of the forest.

'Hello, Wilbur!' I said cheerily. 'Did you have a nice day at wizard school?'

Wilbur didn't reply. Instead, he creased up with laughter.

'What are you wearing?' he asked. 'That dress makes you look like a slug!'

'WILBUR!' I shouted, my bad mood immediately tumbling back with full force. 'I DON'T look like a slug!' I lurched towards him in the air and almost fell off my broomstick.

'Woah!' said Wilbur looking worried for a moment. 'OK, you don't look like a

slug. Let's go home.'

I followed my brother through the air, seething. It had been a (mostly) horrid day and now Wilbur was laughing at my outfit! It *was* a horrible outfit, but still. Why did brothers have to be so *annoying*?

When I got home, I stomped inside without even saying hello to Mum and Dad properly. I wanted to get up to my bedroom where no one could annoy me.

'Why are you wearing that dress Mirabelle?' called Mum as I pushed past her in the porch. 'Did you have an accident at school?'

I didn't answer but ran upstairs to my room and leapt under the covers of my bed . . . too late! I had forgotten that there was a pool of sticky purple goo still on my pillow and now it was all stuck in my hair, AGAIN!'

'ARGH!!!' I yelled, leaping back up again. Today was THE worst day in the history of the world! I would have to wash my hair again and I really couldn't be bothered. I walked across to my window, picking my way over all the clothes and spell ingredients that were strewn across the floor and stared out, putting my chin in my hands. I didn't want to go back downstairs and see my family right now,

but my tummy was rumbling. And where
was Violet? I thought she had followed me
up to my bedroom but now that I looked
around I couldn't see her anywhere.
Hurriedly, I put my hat on my head to hide
the goo and made my way downstairs to
the kitchen. I would try once more to turn
this day around. A chocolate biscuit would

make me feel much better.

'Where's Violet?' I asked, opening the snack cupboard and rummaging for the chocolate biscuits.

'In the sitting room I think,' said Mum. 'Don't eat too many biscuits before dinner, Mirabelle.'

'I won't,' I said. 'I can't find them anyway! Where are they?'

'I think Wilbur took them,' said Mum.

'*Oh*,' I said. 'Where is Wilbur?'

'In the sitting room,' said Mum. 'Are you all right Mirabelle? You seem a bit . . .'

But I didn't hang around to hear what Mum had to say. I whizzed straight out of the kitchen and into the sitting

room where a sight so awful met my eyes
that I almost exploded with rage. Violet
was sitting curled up on the sofa with
Wilbur and he was stroking her. Tiny
purple sparks were fizzing happily from
her snout. And on the coffee table in front
of Wilbur was an *empty* packet of chocolate
biscuits.'

'WILBUR!' I shouted.

Wilbur jumped in surprise and looked around.

'What?' he asked.

'You've eaten ALL the chocolate biscuits!' I shouted.

Wilbur glanced at the empty packet on the table and looked a tiny bit guilty.

'There were only three left,' he said.

'WELL YOU SHOULD HAVE SAVED ONE FOR ME!' I shouted, feeling tears spring to my eyes.

64

'You know they're my favourite biscuits, with the dark chocolate and the jam and the marshmallow and . . .'

Wilbur stared at me, shocked.

'I didn't think,' he said. 'Anyway, I didn't eat ALL three. Violet had half of one.'

Violet looked up at me and now I could see she had chocolate all round her mouth. No wonder she had been so happy cuddling up to Wilbur like that.

'Come to me, Violet,' I said holding my arms out towards her. But Violet just looked at me and blinked.

'Come!' I said, a little more forcefully
now.

'Violet's happy here,' said Wilbur.
'We're watching my wizard's game show.'

'Violet will be happier with me,'
I said. 'She's my dragon after all!'

'Well I think it's unfair that you have a dragon,' said Wilbur. 'Why can't I pet her sometimes?'

'She's MINE,' I said.

'Well she's MINE right now,' said Wilbur. 'I think she prefers me. Look, she doesn't want to come to you anyway.'

'She does,' I said. 'COME Violet!'

Violet blinked and looked a little bit confused but she didn't move from the crook of Wilbur's arm.

'See!' said Wilbur and he looked so smug and pleased with himself in that moment, with chocolate biscuit crumbs all around his mouth, that I thought I would explode with fury! I had had SUCH a bad day and NOBODY understood! I reached into the pocket of my horrible dress and pulled out the tiny bottle of frog potion.

'What are you doing?' asked Wilbur, staring at me suspiciously.

'You'll see!' I said, pulling off the stopper. I felt so cross that I didn't care about getting into trouble any more. Angry mischief bubbled and popped inside me.

Wilbur leapt up off the sofa. He was still holding Violet tightly in his arms.

'If you throw that on

me then it will go on Violet too!' he said.
'So you'd better not!'

'I'm not going to throw it on Violet,'
I said, advancing towards my brother.
'Come to me, Violet. Come!'

Violet was fully awake now. She
wriggled in Wilbur's arms.

'Let her go, Wilbur!' I shouted. 'She
wants to be free!'

'No!' yelled Wilbur, running around
to the other side of the room. I chased
after him. Suddenly, Violet puffed out a
purple flame.

'Oww!' shrieked Wilbur, letting go of
her immediately so that she fluttered up
into the air, snorting indignantly.

Wilbur changed course and started running towards the kitchen.

'Mum! Dad!' he shouted. 'Mirabelle's being naughty!'

It was now or never. I threw my arm back and flung the potion towards Wilbur's back, just as he disappeared through the kitchen door and Dad poked his head around it.

'What's going . . .' he began as the powdery potion whizzed through the air and hit him square in the face.

OOPS.

Chapter FIVE

I stared at Dad in horror and Dad stared
back at me with a shocked expression,
before there was a PUFF of twinkling
smoke. In place of Dad appeared a small
green fairy-frog fluttering in the air and
looking very bewildered. Wilbur stopped
and turned around. When he saw what
had happened he looked VERY smug

and I saw the corners of his mouth twitch. He didn't dare laugh though because now Mum was storming over towards me and she looked FURIOUS.

'MIRABELLE STARSPELL!' she yelled, and I shrank back against the wall. My mum can be really frightening when she gets cross. Suddenly I regretted not caring about my day getting any worse. This was bad. This was *really* bad. I tried to escape by scuttling along the wall.

'STAY WHERE YOU ARE!' Mum
warned, and I stopped scuttling, frozen to
the spot.

'HOW DARE YOU TURN DAD
INTO A FROG!' she shouted, looming
over me.

Wilbur sniggered and Mum whipped
round to glare at him.

'WATCH IT, WILBUR!' she
said, and Wilbur immediately stopped
sniggering and sidled away back into the
sitting room. I took my chance and slid
away from beneath Mum, running out of
the room and towards the stairs. Violet
followed me, her little wings flapping
next to my ear. As I ran I felt tears spring

to my eyes and by the time I got to my
bedroom I could barely see because of
them. I threw myself down on top of my
bed and sobbed into the covers. Violet
nuzzled into my hair. In that moment
it felt as though I couldn't do anything
right.

I cried for what seemed like a
hundred years and then I sat up on my
bed, sniffing, and looked around my room.
It had got dark outside.

'I guess this is our prison now, Violet,'
I said. 'Mum's never going to let us out

of here.' I wiped my eyes and stood up, picking my way over all the things on my floor. It was a very messy prison. I started to pick things up and put them away. If I was never going to be allowed out, I may as well make it look nice in here.

Besides, I definitely needed to change my bed sheets and pillowcase after the purple goo mistake this morning.

By the time I had finished, I actually felt much calmer. It looked really nice in my bedroom. All my things were in their correct places, looking neat and well cared for. I had taken the sheets off my bed and put them in the laundry basket, sneaking out of my room to the airing cupboard to fetch new ones. I still felt a bit cross and a bit sad, but my head felt clearer. I was just sitting down on my new freshly made bed when there was a knock on the door.

'It's the prison warden!' I whispered to Violet and immediately felt a knot of anxiety tighten inside me.

Mum poked her head round the door.
I stared at her and gulped.

'May I come in?' she asked. I didn't
reply but she came in anyway and sat
down beside me on the bed.

'I'm sorry I got so cross with you earlier,' she said. 'I shouldn't have shouted QUITE so much. But really, it was very, very naughty of you to turn Dad into a frog. Luckily the potion didn't last for very long.'

I hung my head. 'I'm sorry. The potion wasn't supposed to go over Dad. It was supposed to go over Wilbur!'

'Well that's hardly the point,' said Mum. 'You shouldn't be throwing potions over anyone.'

'I know,' I said. 'It's just that . . .' and then everything came tumbling out. Everything about my bad, bad day. All the horrible and annoying things that had

happened, starting with the tinsel-hair
potion and finishing up with trying to
turn Wilbur into a frog. I told her about
how I had felt so angry and upset that I
thought I might explode. Mum put her
arm around me.

'I'm sorry you've had such a bad day,' she said. 'Everyone has a bad day now and then, but it's never OK to take it out on the people around you. You must never try and turn your brother into anything, no matter how annoying he is! And I know how annoying big brothers can be. I have two myself.'

'Really?' I said. I couldn't imagine my two kind, funny, and mischievous uncles being annoying at all.

'Oh yes!' smiled Mum.

'So you never tried to turn them into anything?' I asked. 'Or play any tricks on them?'

Mum shuffled uncomfortably on the

bed and I saw her eyes glitter slightly. My mum can be quite naughty too sometimes although she'll never admit it to me.

'Well . . .' she said. 'Er . . . that's not the point, Mirabelle.'

'But Mum . . .' I said.

'No buts!' said Mum holding up her hands. 'The fact is that you should never use your magic to play an unkind trick on someone or to make someone else feel bad. As punishment I'm going to take away your potion kit for a week.'

'A week!' I gasped.

'Yes,' said Mum. 'And I also want you to polish your poor broomstick too. It's in a sorry state.'

'I was going to do that anyway,'
I said. 'I'm going to do it after dinner.'

'Well make sure you keep your
promise this time,' said Mum. 'And you
need to apologize to Dad and Wilbur too.'

'I know,' I said. 'I will.'

'Good,' smiled Mum.

'So where's your potion kit
then?'

I pointed at my
bookshelf where I had
stowed away my potion
kit along with all the
ingredients. Mum looked
surprised.

'It's in its proper place

for once,' she said. 'Well I never!'

'I tidied,' I said.

'Yes I can see that,' said Mum, looking round the room. 'It looks lovely! You'll be much less likely to get into a muddle if you keep things clean and tidy.'

Mum seemed very pleased and for a brief moment I wondered whether she was going to let me keep my potion kit. But instead, she picked it up off the shelf, looked at the clock by my bed and said, 'It's dinner time.'

Chapter SIX

I followed Mum down the stairs and into the kitchen. Dad was serving up spaghetti. My tummy rumbled.

'Dad,' I said. 'I'm really sorry I turned you into a frog.'

'Thank you, Mirabelle,' said Dad. 'It *was* a bit of a shock. Just make sure you don't do it again.'

'I won't,' I promised, and I really
meant it.

Then Wilbur came into the room.

'Wilbur,' I said. 'I'm sorry I *tried* to
turn you into a frog.'

'That's OK,' shrugged Wilbur. 'You failed at it anyway so it's fine.'

I started to feel a prickle of annoyance but then Wilbur said:

'I'm sorry too, Mirabelle. I shouldn't have taken Violet away from you or eaten all the chocolate biscuits or said your dress made you look like a slug.'

I felt a warm glow spread up from my toes.

'That's OK, Wilbur,' I said graciously, and decided to let his comment about me failing to turn him into a frog slide. After all, big brothers just ARE annoying sometimes, aren't they?

We all sat down at the table and began to eat. Violet fluttered onto my lap and curled up, warmly. Everything seemed much brighter and sparklier than it had in the morning, even though it was now completely dark outside. I wanted to make

sure it stayed that way so after dinner I went straight to the cupboard under the stairs and took out my broomstick. I spent a whole hour polishing and brushing it until the handle gleamed and there were no leaves or mud stuck in-between the twigs.

'You've done a great job,' said Mum when she saw it. 'I'm sure your broomstick feels much happier. But now it's time for bed. You had better get that goo washed out of your hair.'

'Oh!' I said, reaching up to touch my hair. I had forgotten about the purple goo. It had hardened up now and felt horrible.

'Do you want me to help?' asked Mum. '*Maybe* we could do that tinsel hair potion together?'

I felt my heart leap.

'Really!' I said.

'I don't see why not,' said Mum. 'Seeing as you've done such a great job tidying your room and polishing your broomstick. You've got to wash your hair anyway so you MAY as well use some tinsel-hair potion on it while you're doing so. It works just like shampoo. I used it a lot when I was younger. I wouldn't mind trying it again . . .'

'Oh Mum,' I said, jumping up and giving her a huge hug. 'I would LOVE that.'

Together we went up the spiral staircase to Mum's witch turret, collecting my book from my bedroom on the way. I love going to the witch turret! It's

where mum does all her potion making. There are shelves full of potion ingredients shimmering and glittering in the light, and in the middle of the room is a big shiny black cauldron.

Mum and I knelt down on the floor and I opened the storybook about the tinsel-haired witch. At the back was the list of potion ingredients to use in case you wanted to make the spell yourself. Mum ran her finger down the list and picked out the bottles we needed. Starshine, a handful of rocketflower petals, liquid soap, and a sprinkling of beetle legs—eww! We weighed and measured the ingredients and then tipped them into the cauldron.

'You stir,' said Mum, handing me the rod.

We said the spell together as I stirred the ingredients round in the cauldron. It started to thicken, becoming pink and bubbly and gloopy. It smelt of soap and flowers.

'Lovely!' said Mum, peering in. 'I think that's ready.' She distilled the mixture into a smaller bottle and then we tidied up and took it downstairs into the bathroom.

'Easier to do it in the bath,' said Mum, turning on the taps.

Once the tub was filled up I hopped into the water, fizzing with excitement. Mum began to wash my hair for me, taking a jug and pouring the water over my head. Then she rubbed some of the potion into my hair. Purple bubbles started to foam all over my head and the whole room smelt of flowers and magic. Bubbles floated in the air all around us, popping and sparkling.

'Ooh,' said Mum, as she rinsed the magic shampoo from my hair. I picked up Dad's shaving mirror from the side of the bath and peered at my reflection. My hair looked beautiful! The purple side of it shimmered and twinkled in the light like strands of lilac tinsel and the other side had gone completely silver.

'I love it!' I said.

Then I got out of the bath and wrapped up in a soft fluffy towel to help Mum do her hair. She leant over the side of the bath and I poured the water over her head, rubbing in the shampoo and washing it off with the jug of water.

'Magnificent!' said Mum, looking in the mirror afterwards. Her hair gleamed and glittered just like mine. We both looked magical and it had felt so nice to do something fun with my mum.

Then it really was time for bed and I skipped back to my bedroom and put on my spider-patterned pyjamas, jumping into bed and snuggling down under the covers with Violet. Mum and Dad came into the room to kiss me goodnight.

'Sweet dreams my glittering little witch,' said Mum.

'Witch-*fairy*,' corrected Dad.

I yawned, sinking down further into my nice clean sheets.

'Goodnight,' I whispered, smiling a big contented smile. My bad day had turned out to be not *quite* such a bad day after all. And I was going to make sure that tomorrow was even better!

Turn the page
for some
mischievous
things to make
and do!

Word Search

```
T F C V R A P E H S B E
I S R S O O H A A N N I
E S P V T C N O T T U Y
R K C I T S M O O R B S
E T O R N A T U G H O A
N N C S G D G R D A H S
R T E Y P O L D K I R A
C S T A R S P E L L H D
A A F F Y R A E W N S E
I R O C R E E M M I U O
T R I S U I I B M S C C
N C B E E H S Y O E R K
```

BROOMSTICK

DRAGON

FROG

KIRA

POTION

SPINDLEWICK

STARSPELL

Witchy Cauldron Cakes

These slime-filled Cauldron Cakes are good enough to eat—they're perfect for a Halloween party or when your witchy friends come round for tea.

(Remember to always ask a grown-up to help when you're baking and make sure to wash your hands before you start.)

Equipment:

* Mixing bowl
* Wooden spoon (or an electric whisk if you have one)
* 12-hole muffin tin
* Scales
* 12 paper cases
* Piping bag (if you don't have one of these, you can improvise with a plastic freezer bag with the corner snipped off with scissors)

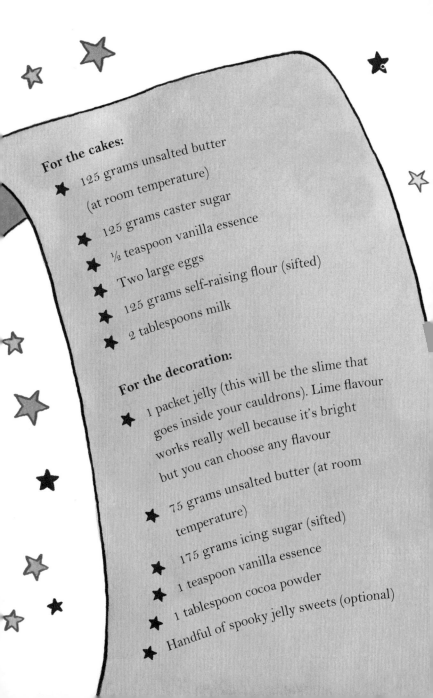

For the cakes:

* 125 grams unsalted butter (at room temperature)
* 125 grams caster sugar
* ½ teaspoon vanilla essence
* Two large eggs
* 125 grams self-raising flour (sifted)
* 2 tablespoons milk

For the decoration:

* 1 packet jelly (this will be the slime that goes inside your cauldrons). Lime flavour works really well because it's bright but you can choose any flavour
* 75 grams unsalted butter (at room temperature)
* 175 grams icing sugar (sifted)
* 1 teaspoon vanilla essence
* 1 tablespoon cocoa powder
* Handful of spooky jelly sweets (optional)

Method:

First, make the jelly according to the packet instructions. You will need to do this the day before you want to make the cakes (as it will need to set overnight in the fridge).

To make the cakes:

1. Preheat the oven to 180C.

2. Mix the butter and sugar together until it is smooth and pale in colour.

3. Add the vanilla essence and mix again.

4. Add one egg and a few spoons of sifted flour. Then add the other egg and the rest of the flour and mix well.

5. Add the milk and mix until smooth.

6. Line your muffin tin with paper cases.

7. Divide the mixture into the cases and bake in the oven for around 15 minutes (but check after 10 minutes).

8. When your cakes are lightly golden, they are ready. Take them out of the oven and leave to cool.

Method:

To decorate:

1. Make the icing by mixing the icing sugar, butter, vanilla essence, and cocoa powder until smooth.

2. Mix up the jelly until it's nice and lumpy.

3. Scoop out a piece from the centre of each cupcake to make a cauldron.

4. Spoon the jelly into the hole in the middle of the cakes.

5. Spoon the icing into a piping bag (or freezer bag with the corner snipped off).

6. Pipe icing around the rim of each cake.

7. If you have some, sprinkle a few jelly sweets onto the green 'slime' in each cauldron for an extra spooky touch.

Witch or fairy quiz

Mirabelle is half witch, half fairy. Her mum,
Seraphina Starspell is a witch but her dad,
Alvin Starspell is a fairy. Mirabelle and
her brother Wilbur are a bit of both,
but which are you?

Answer these questions and find out.

1. What is your favourite day of the year?
   A. Christmas.
   B. Halloween.

2. Which smell do you prefer?
   A. Freshly cut grass.
   B. Bonfire smoke.

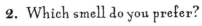

3. When you pick out an outfit do you like to be:

    A. All the colours of the rainbow?

    B. Cool and collected in black?

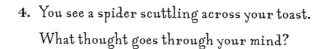

4. You see a spider scuttling across your toast. What thought goes through your mind?

    A. Eeek!

    B. Yummy!

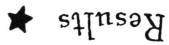 **Results**

Mostly As

You're a fairy through and through! Kind-hearted and at one with nature, you love helping people and spreading a sparkle of joy

Mirabelle
Gets up to Mischief

From the world of ISADORA MOON

MIRABELLE
Gets up to Mischief

Half witch, half fairy, totally naughty!

Harriet Muncaster

Mirabelle
Breaks the Rules

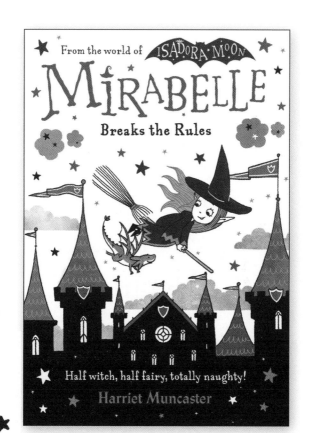

From the world of ISADORA MOON

MIRABELLE
Breaks the Rules

Half witch, half fairy, totally naughty!

Harriet Muncaster

Read more of
Mirabelle's
exciting antics
with Mirabelle
Gets up to
Mischief

Chapter ONE

'NO witchy magic!' said Dad, wagging his finger at me. It was Saturday morning and we were all in the dining room together having breakfast. Me, my mum, my dad, and my brother Wilbur.

'Remember,' said Dad, 'this is a fairy celebration, the most important one in the whole year! I don't want to see any of your

witchy things at the midsummer
dance tonight. No cauldrons, no potion
bottles. No pointy witch or wizard hats!'

'No cauldrons!' I gasped. 'But I
always take my travelling potion kit with
me, wherever I go!'

'I know,' said Dad. 'And it always
seems to cause a lot of mischief.'

'Mischief?' I said trying to look surprised.

'Yes,' said Dad. 'And I don't want any naughtiness at the midsummer's ball this year. You must embrace your fairy side for the night. Why don't you dust off your fairy wand? I never see you using it.'

'That's because it's rubbish!' I complained. 'It only does . . . boring magic.'

Dad raised his eyebrows at me and his fairy wings fluttered in annoyance. I had almost said 'good magic' but stopped myself just in time.

'Dad's right,' chipped in Mum. 'You and Wilbur must embrace your fairy side for the night.' She smiled at us with her dark purple lips. 'You are both half fairy after all.'

Wilbur sighed. He hates being reminded that he's half fairy. He finds it embarrassing and would prefer to be full wizard. I don't mind so much. It can be useful for getting out of trouble. People never expect fairies to be naughty!

'We will *all* do our best to be as "fairy" as possible for Dad,' said

Mum and I stared at her in surprise. Mum is a full blown witch and I could never imagine her trying to be 'fairy,' she loves whisking around on her broomstick and cackling and making potions. Sometimes she can even be quite mischievous too!

'That's settled then!' said Dad. He took a sip of his flower-nectar tea and looked at us all happily over the rim of the mug. Mum crunched down on her spider-sprinkled toast.

I looked back at them and thought about how happy it would make Dad if Wilbur, Mum and I embraced our fairy sides for the night. I decided that I would try my absolute best to be good. No potions, no cauldrons, and no pointed hats!

Harriet Muncaster, that's me! I'm the
author and illustrator of two young fiction
series, Mirabelle and Isadora Moon.
I love anything teeny tiny, anything
starry, and everything glittery.

Love Mirabelle?
Why not try these too . . .